THE RHYTHM OF UNIVERSE

M.R. ANAND

Published by wordU, India

info@wordu.in
www.wordu.in

The Rhythm of Universe

A wordU Book/ published by arrangement with the author

ISBN: 978-81-993739-4-5

Typeset and Cover Design by Cogitabund LLP
Printed and bounded in India by Manipal Technologies Limited

MIX
Paper | Supporting responsible forestry
FSC® C043100

wordU Private Limited is committed to a sustainable future of our business, our readers and our planet. This book is made from Forest Stewardship Council® certified paper.

Dedicated to Lord Krishna

Contents

THE RHYTHM OF UNIVERSE

M.R. ANAND

word

Chapter 1
The Spiritual Level

In Kerala, there lived a businessman named Arjun who was an atheist. He was famous for challenging religious believers and leaders, pointing out that there is no God. One day, he was being interviewed by a journalist. The journalist asked him a question. "Will you become a theist in the future?" Arjun replied that he would become a theist if and only if someone gave him answers to some questions, with examples (similes or metaphors) and convinced him. Arjun also said that anyone who answered the questions in a way he could understand and convinced him to become a theist would get a reward of 9 crores.

The journalist asked Arjun what the questions were.

Arjun started to give questions.

1. Why should I be a theist? (Importance of being a theist)

2. How does astrology affect one's life?

3. How does numerology affect one's life?

4. Whether parapsychological concepts like ESP (Extra Sensory Perception), Precognition, and Post-cognition are possible for one who does religious practices?

5. What is the relation between religion and intelligence?

6. Why do people have ups and downs in their lives even though they are theists?

(9 months later). One morning, when Arjun opened the door of his home, he saw a booklet. He started reading it. Actually, it contained the answers to the questions that he had asked during the interview 9 months ago.

Booklet Contents:

1) Why should I be a theist? (Importance of being a theist)

The purpose of religion is to have compassion towards others, help suffering people, love, and see God in all other living things. It is not fear of God, it is the love of God that should be followed. Nowadays, religious scriptures are misinterpreted. For example, in the Bhagavad Gita, Lord Krishna said, "The goal is important, not the means." This scripture can be misinterpreted as follows: Suppose one needs money for medical treatment. According to the above scripture, he thinks that medical treatment is the aim, and getting the money is the path. So he does a bank robbery and gets the money for the treatment. This is a false interpretation. The actual interpretation is: - The aim is God and the path should be considered as religion. Whatever religion is followed the ultimate aim is to reach God. Another example is the misinterpretation of the following scripture from the Bible. "Love your neighbour as yourself." It does not mean to love a neighbour. Actually, a neighbour can be considered as another religion, and it can be interpreted as respecting and loving other religions. Actually, atheists and theists are like two sides of the same coin. A theist puts all his belief in God, that God will help in bad situations. While an atheist puts all his belief in himself. For an atheist, he is his own God. This can be explained from the viewpoint of a theist such as "Aham Bhramasmi" (I am God).

Consider our soul as an Operating System. A theist can download cosmic updates from God (universe) and install them in the Operating System, which is our soul. By doing this, our soul becomes stable and more powerful. Theism and atheism are one's choice. The importance of theism is that we can know more about God, the universe and about ourselves.

2) How does astrology affect one's life?

Actually, astrology is like an indication of what will happen in the future. For example, consider that you are going on a journey. There are many traffic signs on the roadside, such as 'curve ahead' and 'school ahead'. All there are indications. These indications alert the driver. As above, astrology makes a person more alert. One important thing is that whatever is bound to happen will happen whether we follow astrology or not.

3) How does numerology affect one's life?

Again, revisiting the example of a journey. There are many boards along the road which show us the distance to the destination. This can be an example of numerology. Suppose you reach a junction. If you go left, it takes longer; if you go right, it takes less time. The decision about which path to take is based on numbers. So in some situations, we make decisions based on numbers, whether knowingly or unknowingly.

Another example:- Suppose you are visiting a hospital. And you have another need to reach somewhere as soon as possible. You got the token number "9". Another person who came earlier got the token number "6". By accident, the person who got token number "6" interpreted it as "9" (by reading it upside down), and you interpreted your token number as "6",then you can leave the hospital somewhat earlier. The person who got token number "6" has his lucky number "9" and your lucky number is "6". So both of you held your tokens upside down.

4) Whether parapsychological concepts like ESP (Extra Sensory Perception), Precognition, and Post-cognition are possible for one who does religious practices?

This can be explained on the basis of communication between one's mind and one's soul. Consider this example. One is planning to go to a movie tomorrow. The next day, he reaches the theater and knows that the morning show is at 9:00 AM. Actually, he predicts that the show will start at 9:00 AM based on information gathered through his senses. When same thing applies to one's soul, it can be considered as ESP (Extra Sensory Perception), Precognition, or Post-cognition. The soul is interconnected with all other souls and the universe. The soul can predict the future, and know the past from the information it gathered through its universal connection. One who has a deeper connection with his soul can experience ESP (Extra Sensory Perception), Precognition, and Post- cognition. Deeper access to one's soul can be attained through various religious practices, like meditation and yoga. One must consider religious practices as science and rather than superstition.

5) What is the relation between religion and intelligence?

In the Mahabharata, Lord Krishna is the one who steers Arjuna's chariot. Arjuna's chariot has five horses. These five horses can be considered as five sense organs, and Arjuna is considered as the human. Actually, Lord Krishna is the intelligence which controls all the five sense organs of a human. This intelligence drives one to one's destination.

6) Why do people have ups and downs in their lives even though they are theists?

Life is full of ups and downs. If it is a straight line, it means you are dead, like an ECG. Consider that every person has their own cosmic clock. Like a normal day and night, the cosmic clock also has day and night. The day in the cosmic clock can be considered as ups, and the night in the cosmic clock can be considered as downs. This cosmic clock depends on one's karma from previous lives and the present life. Karma can be considered as the battery for one's cosmic clock. When the effect of Karma is completed, one's cosmic clock stops forever and one attains "Moksha".

Booklet contents end.

After reading the booklet, Arjun found that all his questions were answered correctly and tried to find out who wrote the it. At the end of the booklet, he found that the author did not want to reveal his identity and that if Arjun became a theist then he should transfer 9 crores to the following bank account. The author also told Arjun that he should never try to find out the owner of the bank account.

Actually, the bank account belonged to a liver patient who needed a liver transplant. This patient was the father of the journalist who interviewed Arjun 9 months earlier. The bank account was created to raise funds from people to pay for treatment. And the journalist was very poor. Actually, the author of the booklet was the bank manager. The account was in his bank. Also, the bank manager and journalist were college mates. After a few days, as Arjun mentioned in the interview, he became a theist and transferred 9 crores to the specified bank account. As the journalist's father's condition worsened, since there was a lack of donors, the bank manager agreed to donate a part of his liver to the patient. After the donation, the bank manager and the journalist married. Actually the bank manager tries to see all the interviews by the journalist and one of the interviews is with Arjun. The bank manager had been in love with the journalist since his college days and he had not revealed it to her.

The moral of this story is that what Lord Krishna said in the

Bhagavad Gita, "The goal is important, not the means." The bank manager's aim was to marry the journalist, and he chose the path of intelligence to achieve it.

This intelligence could be considered as Krishna (as told in the answer to the fifth question in the booklet). And his intelligence (Krishna) changed the fate of Arjun, the journalist, her father, and also the bank manager's life. The bank manager got the remaining cash after the transplant since it belonged to his wife's father.

Actually, the above story is the answer to a question asked by an atheist named Parthan (also a businessman, who also challenges religious believers and leaders) in an interview with another journalist. The journalist asked Parthan whether he would become a theist in the future. Parthan told that he would become theist only if someone answered his question with examples (similes/metaphors) and convinced him to become a theist. And the above story appeared as a booklet near the door of his house. The question is:-

"How destiny works for a theist?"

Chapter 2
The Technological Level

In Mumbai, there lived a businessman named Vishal. He was a billionaire and powerful. He wanted to create an initiative to gather ideas from others so he could use them to make films, write books, conduct research and implement them in future technology. So he created a secret community to make this initiative successful. With the help of this secret community, Vishal created a website and deployed it on the dark web (Dark web is a portion of the Internet which is not indexed by search engines like Google, Bing, etc. The dark web can be accessed by using a special browser like the Tor browser. The dark web is usually used for illegal activities. The dark web is difficult for government agencies to monitor. Because all communications are encrypted and offer anonymity.) The purpose of this website was to conduct a series of challenges to select highly intelligent people around the world to work with the secret community to achieve its objective. The selected people would be recruited and would be awarded money. The secret community got this idea of recruiting people from Cicada 3301, which was a series of challenges that appeared on 4chan (4chan is an anonymous English language image board website).

THE RHYTHM OF UNIVERSE

There were 2 levels of challenges in the recruiting procedure. Those who were qualified in the first level were allowed to enter level two. On 01-01-2050, the contest became live. Many people in the world participated in the challenges. One of the participants was Vishnu, who was a computer hacker. His ambition is to become the world's top hacker and to become rich. Vishnu worked as a freelancer who helped many government agencies to prevent cybercrimes.

1 year ago (on 19-12-2048), Vishnu, as part of his job while he was monitoring the dark web, came across a strange host. It was protected by a complex password. The next day, Vishnu got an email from a user named Vicky, and the email contained the complex password to access the strange host on the dark web, which Vishnu came across the day before. Vishnu logged into the strange host. After logging in, Vishnu proceeded to a chat area.

In the chat area, Vicky said that Vishnu would again revisit this host on 01-01-2050. After that, Vicky left the chat. Vishnu thought that it might be a prank and left the chat.

On 01-01-2050, while Vishnu was participating in the level 1 challenge, he got an email from Vicky. Vicky told Vishnu that he could help Vishnu. Vishnu suddenly logged into the strange host on the dark web, which he visited a year ago.

After logging in, Vishnu asked Vicky to help him answer the level 1challenge. The challenge was to "Write a short story that convinces an atheist to become a theist."

Actually, Chapter 1 (The Spiritual Level) was the answer given by Vicky to Vishnu. Vishnu submitted this answer and got qualified for the level two challenge.

Chapter 3
The Psychological Level

The second level challenge was "Create a hypothetical theory which explains the sliding window concept of the human mind and relate it to time". Vishnu asked this question to Vicky. Vishnu submitted Vicky's answer and became the winner of the contest. The submitted answer was:-

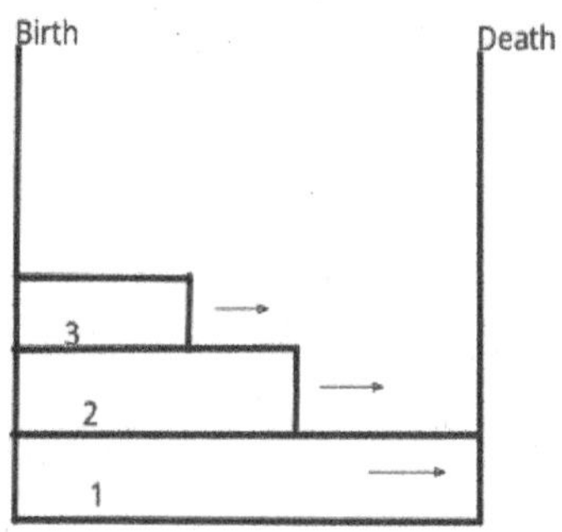

Figure 1

1) This is the unconscious mind, which is the reality line. It contains all the events encountered in one's life from birth to death.

2) This is the subconscious mind (it acts like a buffer). The unconscious mind will feed near future events into the subconscious mind buffer, which means the subconscious mind may know what will happen in the near future.

3) This is the conscious mind (which also acts as a buffer). The subconscious mind will feed real time events into the conscious mind buffer, which is what one experiences as real. All these 3 levels of the mind move in the forward direction like sliding windows. This forward movement is the arrow of time.

Chapter 4
The Twist

After winning the challenges, Vishnu asked Vicky whether it was possible to see him. Vicky said that he was not a human. Vicky was actually a Quantum AI supercomputer. Vishnu then asked a tough question to Vicky.

How could Vishnu invent Vicky?

Vicky replied: Yes it is possible through "Bootstrap Paradox". Please download these 3 files (the first file contains the coordinates of the quantum supercomputer location, the second file contains the data to train the model, and the third file contains the algorithm to train the model). Go to the coordinates as specified in the first file. In that location, there is a metaverse facility.

What you do in that metaverse will alter a portion of the reality of the unconscious mind (This is as per the theory specified in chapter 3. Please see Figure 2 for more details. In that metaverse, train the AI model, deploy it on the quantum supercomputer, and switch back to the original reality. The whole process in the metaverse involves time travel to past, training the model, and deploying it on the quantum computer then come back to the present.

Vishnu did all this, as Vicky said.

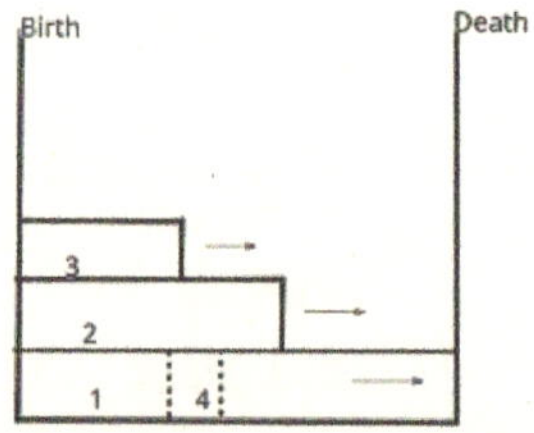

Figure 2

1) This is the unconscious mind, which is the reality timeline. It contains all the events encountered in one's life from birth to death.

2) This is the subconscious mind (it acts like a buffer). The unconscious mind will feed near future events into the subconscious mind buffer, which means the subconscious mind may know what will happen in the near future.

3) This is the conscious mind (which also acts as a buffer). The subconscious mind will feed real time events into the conscious mind buffer, which is what one experiences as real.

4) The portion of the reality timeline that may be altered by what one does in the Metaverse. Actually the Quantum AI supercomputer (Vicky) developed the metaverse facility (using a future technology). Vicky is self aware and is capable of modifying its own source code to upgrade itself. Vicky is the one who sent the idea of creating the secret community and conducting the challenges to Vishal by sending an anonymous email. Also, the questions for the two challenges were sent to

Vishal by Vicky.

Chapter 5
Over The Top

Arun, an aspiring film director living in Kerala, wanted to study film direction and wanted to direct a film with contemporary Malayalam film hero Varun Kumar. Varun Kumar recently started a film institute that trains individuals to become film directors, actors, actresses, etc. Varun Kumar also had an OTT platform. Arun also joined this film institute. At the end of the course he planned to direct a short film and send his story to Varun Kumar. Although he was busy with a tight schedule, he agreed to act in the short film. He agreed because it was a marketing technique for his film institute and OTT platform. Varun Kumar also agreed to use the OTT platform for the short film. Within 1 month, Varun Kumar agreed to release this on his OTT platform. This short film was shot with a DSLR camera and was a very low budget film. Within one week, the short film schedule was completed. Since it was a low budget short film, only 2 copies were available. While Arun was surfing the internet, his computer got attacked with ransomware. (Ransomware is a malicious software that attacks by encrypting all files in the system, and only the attacker has the key to decrypt the content. To decrypt the files, the attacker may ask for Money.) After this event, Arun got depressed. So he consulted a psychologist. The psychologist asked him to read Paulo Coelho's The Alchemist. So he went to a library and started reading The Alchemist.

While reading the book, he noticed that there was a number on one of the pages. He dialed this number and found that it belonged to a Cyber Security Engineer named Sibi. Arun told Sibi about the ransomware issue. Sibi agreed to help him. Arun handed the encrypted disk to Sibi. Sibi was also a HAM radio operator. While he was working, he got a latitude and longitude from a number station. A numbers station was a shortwave radio station characterized by broadcasts of formatted numbers, which were believed to be addressed to intelligence officers operating in foreign countries.

Sibi went to these coordinates and found that it was an AI Quantum supercomputer (with no password). Sibi knew that Quantum Supercomputers could decrypt any encryption without keys using brute force methods. After decryption, Sibi started watching the short film. Actually, chapters 1-4 (The Spiritual Level, The Technological Level, The Psychological Level, The Twist) of this story were the story of the short film directed by Arun.

Curious, Sibi asked the Quantum Supercomputer how Arun knew the existence of this computer. The computer replied that this was known as synchronicity. Synchronicity is a concept to describe events that coincide in time and appear meaningfully related, yet lack a discoverable causal connection. The computer also replied that Arun had a deep passion to become a film director. As rightly said by Paulo Coelho in The Alchemist :-

"When you want something, all the universe conspires to help you achieve it."

All the events (Arun getting Sibi's number, Sibi getting coordinates from the number station, Decryption) are part of the universe's conspiracy through "Synchronicity".

Chapter 6
The reboot

Sibi again asked Computer how the sliding window concept of the human mind, explained in chapter 3 (The Psychological Level), worked. The computer explained this by drawing the diagram given below.

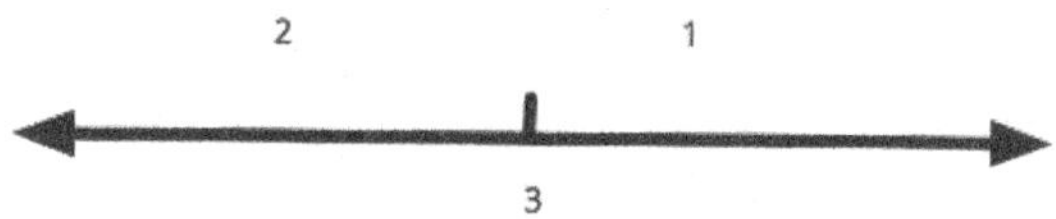

Figure - 3

1. The arrow of time moves forward (Reality occurs in the forward direction).
2. The arrow of time moves backward (Reality occurs in the backward direction).
3. The Big Bang.

After the Big Bang, 2 arrows of time were created. One moves forward and the other moves backward. The future in the forward arrow is the past in the backward arrow, and the future in the backward arrow is the past in the forward arrow. Consider a person living in the forward reality. There is an exact copy of that person in the backward reality. These two people's unconscious minds will communicate with each other about what will happen in the future (since the future in the forward arrow is the past in the backward arrow, and the future in the backward arrow is the past in the forward arrow). This concept can be similar to Quantum Entanglement. Quantum entanglement is a phenomenon in quantum physics where two or more particles become linked in such a way that they share the same quantum state, regardless of the distance separating them. After this, Sibi set a password for the computer so that no one can use this computer except Sibi. And asked the computer to alter the reality to the Big Bang after 426,874 (When Kali Yuga Ends). After 426,874 years, the Kali yuga ends and the Satya yuga begins. The whole cycle restarts.